I0567674

Still Waters Burn Deep

A Short Story

By Pebbles Lacasse

Previously published as part of the anthology
Quarantined: A Boxed Set of Pandemic Proportions

Bonus story:
A Run with Charley

STILL WATERS BURN DEEP

© 2021 Pebbles Lacasse

ISBN 978-1-989979-14-3

Cover design © 2021 cover artist T.A. Moorman
Anthology Edition March 2021
Standalone Edition ©Pebbles Lacasse February 2022
Published by Pebbles Lacasse
https://www.pebbleslacasse.com

Chapter One

Mmm, bacon.

Wait, what?

I jolt from sleep, wide awake and terrified. Why do I smell food cooking? I live alone.

As quietly as I can, I slip out of bed, avoiding the creaks in the floor that will alert my intruder. Ever so slowly, I open my closet door and reach up, and feel for the cold hard steel I keep loaded, just in case.

The gap between the door and its frame make for a great peephole but I see nothing.

I hear the drag sound of a plate being taken from the cupboard and then being placed on the counter.

My heart pounds in my ears and my hands shake as I remove the safety on my 9mm. I close my eyes and take a deep, calming breath before I leap out from behind the door, gun pointed toward the kitchen.

The gun suddenly feels heavy, weighing down my arms until it is no longer a threat to my intruder, or should I say, my husband's oldest friend.

He wears a pair of old, faded blue jeans with slightly shredded hems. His army green shirt is a snug fit, accentuating his well-toned physique. Although his dark hair is slightly receding and much shorter than I remember it to be, he's still just as sexy as ever.

"Jordan, what the fuck are you doing here? I could've shot you!"

He takes his time turning around, places two eggs on a plate, then looks at me as he sets it on the table.

"Are you going to join me or shall I eat alone?"

Jordan is a sexy man. I've always found him desirable, even though I married his best friend fourteen years ago.

When I was twenty, I met Jordan at *Lulu's Diner* where I worked as a waitress. He said his name was Jerry. The way his eyes followed me as I cared for other patrons had my pussy slick and ready. I wanted him more than I'd ever wanted any man.

I shake my head to escape the memory.

"How did you get in here?" I said in a sharp and angry tone.

His eyes scan my body before he turns to load another plate and set it on the table. He points to the one, suggesting it's for me.

He sits and holds up a key dangling from a keychain sporting a beer bottle charm. "David gave me a key for emergencies."

"How does breakfast count as an emergency?" I ask.

I walk back to my room to put the gun away, checking twice to ensure the safety has been activated.

"We are in a state of emergency." He sips from his mug. "Have you not watched the news? The world is in quarantine."

I stand against the wall, keeping a fair distance from him. "Yeah, I've heard, but what the fuck are *you* doing here?" I pause. "Social Distancing, have you heard of it? You shouldn't be here. What if you're infected?"

He points to the plate he made for me. "Please, sit. I've been in quarantine for two weeks already. I've seen nobody and didn't stop anywhere while I was making the trip here. It's unlikely I have the virus."

His gruff voice makes me recall our fling as if it happened last week, even though it was sixteen years ago.

After I'd gotten off work, he took me to his apartment and we spent the next three hours having the hottest, naughtiest sex I'd ever had the pleasure of experiencing. When I left, I didn't ask for his number nor did I offer him mine. I knew it was a one-time thing, but it will always be one of the most dangerous, irresponsible things I'd ever done. He was my one and only one-night stand.

Six months later, I saw him standing across the street. We stared at each other for a long time. He was with a man, but I don't recall looking directly at him. His eyes held my attention until I gained the courage to walk away. I looked back and saw him trying to find a break in traffic so he could pursue me. I rushed down the street and slipped into a restaurant where I hid in the bathroom for half an hour until I was sure he'd given up and left the area.

Not talking to him that day became one of my biggest regrets.

Two years later, I met my husband, David, and two years after that we were to be married. The day before the wedding, the best man, someone he had only ever glowered about, showed up on our doorstep. Low and behold, it was my one-night stand.

I nearly fell over. For whatever reason, I didn't tell my husband I knew him. My fling said nothing either.

With my hands on my hips, I scoff, "How do you know I'm safe?"

He chuckles. "You rarely leave the house anymore."

He's right. I've been a homebody ever since David died, last year. He couldn't have children, so it's just me living here in isolation. I like it this way but it can be lonely, at times. Sometimes, I swear I can feel David standing beside me and it leaves me feeling empty. I want the impossible; I want him back.

"You don't know me." I pull out the chair and sit across from him. "You haven't been here in ten years." I sip the black coffee he poured for me. My anger burns under the surface of my cool exterior. "He died last year. Did you know?"

He looks up at me with seductive dark brown eyes. "Yes, I knew."

"Where the fuck were you... when I needed someone?" I glare into his sultry eyes. I drop my gaze when the faded image of him looking down at me while he fucked me fills my thoughts.

"I was overseas." He sips his coffee and leans back in his chair. "I didn't know until I called my sister. By the time my tour was up too much time had passed."

I pick up my fork and fiddle with it, trying to make it feel right in my hand. The tines dip into the egg yolk and it seeps onto a strip of bacon.

"I didn't know you were overseas." My eyes meet his. "Thank you for your service."

He grumbles in his humble manner.

"I was only halfway through my tour when he passed."

He inhales deeply, releasing slowly. His head hangs and I can't see his face. He snuffs before wiping his eyes.

Is he crying?

"Are you okay?" I ask with a soothing voice. I'm sure he misses David, maybe as much as I do.

"I miss him," Jordan whispers. "It doesn't help that he died before we could resolve our issues."

He looks up at me and trails of tears grace his dark chocolate cheeks. He quickly wipes them away and snuffs again before picking up his fork and aggressively stabbing at his food, shoving bite after bite into his mouth.

"Well, you ran off before you two could talk it out. And why didn't you tell him you were leaving to go fight in a war?" I stand and toss my full plate on the counter, spilling eggs over its edge. "Unresolved issues…" I pause. "No kidding! How do you think he would have felt if you had died and not him?"

He replies with a raised voice. "Probably the same way I feel about the fact that he died and left me with unresolved issues."

I jump to my feet and make my way towards the bathroom. "He wasn't driving the car. It wasn't his fault. He didn't die on purpose!" I slam the door.

He yells, "I'm sorry, but I couldn't face him." I hear his chair slide on the hardwood floor. "He would have wanted to know everything and you know it."

He's right. Telling David the whole story would have crushed him. There are secrets I took to his grave.

Chapter Two

The bathroom door allows for some much-needed distance from the hot mess in my kitchen. My shower consists mostly of me crying until the water runs cold. I emerge from the bathroom to discover he tidied the kitchen. He's nowhere to be seen.

Disappointment washes over me. Once again, he disappears without a word. Sure, I wasn't very cordial, but what did he expect after he broke David's heart? He has the nerve to reappear only after he's been long buried! Is he hoping to continue what we stared, so many years ago?

Not a fucking chance!

After I dress and my damp hair is pulled into a messy bun, I pour a fresh mug of coffee. With the mug in one hand, and a book in the other, I make my way to the patio.

The sun's warmth instantly surrounds me, comforting me with an invisible hug. My skin livens as the sunrays kiss my flesh.

"Are you going to stand there all day?"

I jolt, spilling some coffee on my fluffy yellow slippers. "You fucking scared me!"

He snickers. "How did you not see me sitting here?"

With my book held over my eyes like a visor blocking the blinding sunlight, I'm able to open my lids without pain. He's sitting on the lounge chair, shirtless, coffee mug in hand.

A light layer of sweat livens his dark skin, accentuating every hill and valley of muscle on his bare chest. He has the body of a fit Marine capable of taking on any enemy in hand-to-hand combat.

"Well, are you going to sit?"

I pull my chair until it rests several feet from his. "Isn't there someone else you could be bothering?"

"Probably, but there isn't anyone else I'd rather be locked up with during a pandemic."

He watches me, waiting for me to respond. Instead, I open my book and read.

"You should take off that t-shirt and get some colour on that lily-white skin of yours."

I roll my eyes and shake my head. "You'd like that, wouldn't you?"

He snickers then returns his attention to his book.

Half an hour later, I look over at him and see that he's fallen asleep. If I were cruel, I'd throw my empty mug at him. He did look tired. He said he drove here without stopping anywhere. Does that mean he drove an entire day without taking a break? It's no wonder he's asleep.

His hand rests just above the bulge in his jeans, the opposite arm lies over his face, shielding his eyes. Years ago, he was posed just like this when I took him in my mouth, devouring inch after thick inch of his cock. Not letting me make him cum, he grabbed me under my arms and yanked me up his body. I straddled him, slipped him inside me and rode him until we both erupted in orgasm.

Well, that was then and this is now. Things have changed.

"Stop staring at me," he grumbles, lifting his arm to peer at me.

I shift. "I'm not."

"Yes, you were." Jordan sits up, using his shirt to wipe the sweat from his chest and forehead. "Do you like what you see?"

"Stop that!" I hiss.

He chuckles. "Don't worry, I'm not here to seduce you."

"So, why are you here?" I slam my book shut.

"When I stood beside David as he said his vows to you, I promised to care for you should he ever not be here to do so." He stands, massive shoulders block the sun from my face. "As his best man, it's my duty."

Why can't Jordan be a disgusting man who burps and farts every other minute? He's hot, sexier than he used to be, and a gentleman hoping to play the role of my saviour.

"It's not the early nineteen-hundreds. I don't need saving. I'm quite capable of caring for myself." I stand and storm into the house, shutting the patio door behind me. I set the mug in the sink and then put my book back on the nightstand.

"Ally," he calls to me from the living room. I don't reply but he finds me in my bedroom. "I know you don't need saving. You're tougher than I could ever hope to be."

I concur. "You're damn right I am."

"I haven't been there for you, and it's about time that changes. My whole life I've been a runner. When things get tough I flee. After I saw you on the street, all those years ago..." he pauses and his eyes scan my body. "Well, I had joined the Army."

My heart sinks as regret washes over my soul. I should have talked to him that day and not hidden in that bathroom.

He gradually steps closer to me. "On your five-year wedding anniversary, when David saw me lean in to kiss you, I should have stuck around to help smooth things over. Like a coward, I volunteered to deployed overseas to avoid him."

"What the hell were you thinking? He was furious about that kiss, claiming it looked like we were lovers and not two people who'd just met. It was months before he stopped questioning me about that. I had to lie to him to convince him that it was just a stupid thing that happened because we were both drinking, and lost our heads." I take a breath and shake my head. "He didn't need to know we have a history."

Jordan attempts to take my hand but I back away toward the bed to get some distance. He pursues, forcibly taking my hand. It looks so tiny in his huge grasp.

"When David died, I should have come home, but I didn't. I couldn't. So much has happened between us that I should have handled better." I pull my hand from him as he continues his confession. "I love you. I've loved you for a long time."

"Yes, I know," I snap. "You made sure to tell that to David when he caught you kissing me. I told him you were drunk and out of your head."

His voice rises. "As I recall, you didn't push me away from that kiss. You wanted me to kiss you until you realized David saw us."

"Fine! Yes, I did. I wanted you to kiss me. I wanted you that night, but I would never have acted on those desires, had you not tried to seduce me. But by you telling him you love me, that really fucked things up. It's like you were purposely trying to ruin my marriage and destroy your best friend in the process." I jab my finger into his chest. "You hurt him, and I lied to him to protect our secret. You putting me in that position was a shitty thing to do." I shove him aside as I attempt to leave the bedroom.

He grabs my wrists and pulls my back against his chest. He pins my arms over my heaving breasts, my back presses against his strong chest. I battle to get free, but I cannot escape his embace. It takes a few minutes, but I finally give in and sag into him, tears seep down my cheeks.

I whisper. "We hurt him that day. We broke his heart. I'll never forgive myself for that."

"It was my fault. I never should have kissed you." He takes a deep breath, releasing it slowly. "If I weren't such a coward, I would have gotten your number before letting you walk out of my apartment, all those years ago. I've regretted it every day since. I knew you were special, and yet, I let you go."

I reassure him. "It was never supposed to be more than it was."

He spins me, still not setting my arms free. "But there was more to it. Right?"

"Yes, as it turns out, there was."

He tenderly wipes the tears that spill from my eyes.

He leans down, pausing before his lips touch mine as if asking for permission. Something in my eyes must reveal the answer he's seeking. Be it a moment or an eternity, my soul begs my heart to put a stop to this. But its efforts are futile.

Chapter Three

Our lips touch and every fibre in my being swoons. I've given in to the hunger. His tongue parts my lips. The tenderness of his kiss erupts into a heated passion, so hot neither of us can stop the fires that burn.

Jordan yanks off my sweatshirt. One arm wraps around my back and lifts me, the other lowers us to the bed. My arms embrace his back, holding him against me, releasing only when he slips down my body. He leaves a trail of sensuous kisses from each breast, leading down to my tummy.

His fingers grip the waistband of my pants and tug them off. In a flash, his mouth engulfs my heated folds, swallowing me up.

Oh, fuck, yes!

His mouth sucks at my flesh while flicking on my swollen clitoris with his fat tongue. *I don't want to cum yet.* Desire burns my core as my need to have him inside me becomes overwhelming. My hands grab at his shoulders, urging him without words to give me what I need.

His mouth presses to mine as his thick, beefy cock slowly fills me. My walls stretch to accommodate. Our moans drown in each other's mouths and my thoughts begin to fade away.

His body slaps against mine as I grab at his flesh, my nails dig into his back. Our heated passion yearns of urgency, as though trying to make up for years of missed moments.

My orgasm grows, quick to wash over me as his chest presses heavier onto mine.

His hand weaves into my hair as the other grasps my hip. With his cheek pressed against mine, the heat of his whimpered breaths warm my ear.

"I fucking love you," he whispers.

His tempo slows as he nears his climax, thus giving us a moment to savour each other. Our lips meet again and our tongues dance. My lengthy moan is met with his whimper.

Jordan's hand glides along my superheated flesh and rests on my cheek. His lips lift from mine and he cries out. I watch his handsome face contort into a pained orgasmic expression.

His body stiffens above me. His prick swells and twitches inside me as his muscles jerk. His breath holds then releases with a long, satiated moan.

His lips return to mine, but I slowly turn my face away. Guilt now plagues me, tearing at my soul. David is dead. I know this, so why does it feel like I've just cheated on him?

"Get off," I hiss, pushing his shoulders when he doesn't immediately move.

Jordan rolls over with a confused expression, making me wonder why he isn't ashamed for having sex with his best friend's wife. Dead or not, this should pull at his heartstrings. Shouldn't it? Maybe I'm being overly sensitive. Should I live without flesh-on-flesh contact for the rest of my life?

"I can't do this."

My words cause him to bolt upright. He reaches for me but I'm quick to come to my feet.

"What? What are you talking about?" He stands and walks around the bed to get closer to me but I avoid him. "Why are you being like this? We had a nice moment there. I don't underst—"

I cut him off. "This is wrong! I'm married to David, who is supposedly your best friend, or have you forgotten?"

He stands tall, frustration riddling his expression. "David is dead! He won't mind."

"You don't know that!" I shout.

I pick up my clothing and rush from the bedroom, slamming the bathroom door and flip the lock. I can hear the creaking of the floor beneath his footsteps as he approaches.

He calls through the door when his attempt to open it fails. "Why are you being this way?"

"Leave me alone," I reply while starting the shower.

He yells. "I'm here! David's not! I'm not going anywhere, so you'd better get used to it."

I can't think of anything to say that will make him leave. But do I really want him to go? I can't erase what just happened. It felt good to be touched.

My heart died with David and I have no desire to resurrect it. I don't want Jordan to go, but I don't want him to   stay   either.

Chapter Four

After a quick shower, I wrap myself in a towel and open the bathroom door. I expect Jordan to be standing there waiting, but he's not. I don't see him anywhere and his truck is exactly where he parked it, so he couldn't have gone far.

Part of me is angry that he didn't get in his truck and leave. Another part of me is grateful that my freak-out didn't scare him away. I need to get better control of my emotions.

What happened between Jordan and me so many years ago still haunts at me every day. The memories plague me despite my efforts to pretend it never happened.

I hesitate with the fridge door open and wonder if I should make dinner for one or two. The least I can do is feed him, if he returns. The poor man has an orgasm and then is hit with my emotional tsunami.

Half hour later, the patio door slides open and my heart pounds harder in my chest. He cautiously approaches me.

Without turning around, I ask, "Are you hungry?"

He clears his throat. "I could eat."

Neither of us moves. Silence fills the room.

He sighs. "About earlier…"

I quickly stop him. "I don't want to talk about it. Sit, we'll eat."

"I *am* going to talk and you're going to listen." He pauses and watches me load a plate high with spaghetti. "If you aren't ready for what happened earlier, just say so, and I won't pursue physical intimacy until you're ready. When you are, you can let me know."

"Who says I'm ever going to be ready, or whether I even care to have sex with you again?" I hand him his plate without meeting his gaze.

"I love you enough to wait." He sits at the table.

I whisper. "My heart belongs to another."

"Well, provided the virus doesn't invade my body and kill me, I won't be going anywhere."

We eat the rest of the meal in silence. Afterward, I sit on the sofa and read my book while he unloads supplies from his truck. He takes his time organizing the food in the cupboards and pantry. When he finishes, he showers. We haven't said a word to each other.

I slip on my nightgown and brush my hair, tying it back in a long French braid.

I emerge from the bedroom to see that he's had a shower and stands in the kitchen with a towel around his waist. The man is ripped with muscle. His back is shaped like a V with wide shoulders and a small waist. His arms are thick but ankles are thin below shapely calves. The towel does nothing to hide his round, firm buttocks that fit so perfectly in my hands while he filled me, earlier.

The ambient lighting amplifies the mountains of back muscle as he lifts his arm to drink. His skin glistens with beads of water droplets. I want to touch him. I take two

17

silent steps toward him before the floor creaks. He turns around and meets my eyes, halting me in place.

"You checking me out is becoming a habit," he teases. "Do you like what you see?"

I do. I really do!

"A wet man dripping on my kitchen floor?" I roll my eyes and head to the fridge to pour myself a glass of *Pinot Grigio*. "Do you want a glass of wine?"

"Do you have beer?" he says as he turns to face me.

My eyes instinctively drop to the mound beneath the towel, but I quickly avert them. I dig near the back of the fridge.

"I have two cans. They've been in here for a while, so please drink them."

I try to walk away but his strong hand slides up my arm, and I freeze.

He insists, "Don't shut me out. We can at least be friends. Can't we?"

I shrug and sip my wine, still not turning to face him.

"We never had a chance to talk about the, um—" He pauses. "David was always around. It was obvious you hadn't told him about us, about the um... the *thing*." He takes a breath and releases my arm. "It wasn't my place to—"

I cut him off. "No, it wasn't your place!"

Jordan holds up his hands in surrender. "That's why I didn't say anything."

My voice softens. "Thank you for keeping the secret." I shift my weight nervously and take a big gulp of wine. "I'm sure if he'd known, it would have broken him. We wouldn't have recovered from that."

"Can we talk about it?" he asks, seeming sincere. "I mean, *really* talk about it."

I reply with a heavy sigh. "It's water under the bridge."

"A baby isn't water."

Chapter Five

"You knew?" My stomach drops out, leaving me to feel hollow.

His eyebrows nearly meet. "I saw you on the street that day. Your hand was resting on your bloated belly. It didn't take a master's degree to figure it out."

I gulp my wine and refill the glass, and then walk to the living room and sit on the sofa. He follows, sits at the opposite end, and sets his beer on the table.

"Yes, I was pregnant—" I pause to watch my finger trace the edge of the glass. "And she was yours."

He whispers. "A girl?"

I nod and sip from my glass, set it on the table, and then lean back on the sofa.

He asks, "But, why did you run from me? I would've helped you with anything you needed. I would've been there for you. I went to the place we met—your work—and they said you'd quit. I had no idea how to find you, and they wouldn't tell me."

"You were a one-night stand. I wasn't about to burden you with a child. Besides, she was mine, not yours. Maybe I was wrong in my thinking. I don't know. The last thing I wanted was to stress myself out with a new relationship."

"We didn't have to start a relationship. We could have been co-parents, or whatever the term is."

I stand and glide over to the patio doors and look out into the blackness of the night.

"Well, as it turns out, parenting wasn't in the cards for either of us." I look at him, arms crossed over my chest to protect my heart. "I'm glad you didn't have to experience that. Nothing comes close to the pain of losing a child that never got to take a single breath."

He glides toward me. "I was there at the hospital after you gave birth."

I gasp and spin. "What?"

I'm numb. I feel nothing but emptiness as he tells me his story.

"I couldn't bring myself to go into your room." He shakes his head as if filled with regret. "I calculated the approximate time you'd deliver. My aunt's best friend is a nurse in obstetrics. She was watching for labouring mothers named Ally that matched the description I gave her of you. It was probably against their privacy rules. Nonetheless, she called when you came in."

My arms hug my hollow body as my reflection in the window reveals the tears that spill down my cheeks.

"I went to the hospital to see you, but when I asked where you were…" He pauses and runs his hand over his face before he continues. "They told me what happened. She took me to your room, but when I looked in and saw how broken you were, I knew I would only make the most horrible moment in your life even worse. I sat on the floor outside your door for three hours, listening to you cry."

"You shouldn't have been there."

He clears his throat. "I did that to you. You were there because of me. I'll never forgive myself for not walking through that door and taking some of that burden from you. I was a coward. I should have let you yell at me, blame me, hit me, or cry on my shoulder. I wasn't there for you."

He stands behind me, his warm hands on my shoulders. His cheek rests on my head. I want him to hold me, to take away the reminder of the day that forever broke me in two.

"And when David died, I wasn't here. I left you to carry the pain alone." He kisses the top of my head. "So, I had to get to you to protect you during this pandemic. I will live up to my promise to David and keep you safe."

I spin and rise on my toes and kiss him. I need comfort and this is how I will get it.

He whispers. "Use me how you will. Hate me if you need to. I will be forever on my knees before you."

"Take me," I reply.

Chapter Six

Jordan's mouth presses to mine with undeniable passion. I lean against the patio door while he sinks to his knees.

He lifts my nightie and laps at my folds; his tongue jutting feverishly over my clitoris. I spread my legs more, giving him easier access. He grips my ass and pulls my hips forward. His fat tongue savours my arousal while sucking and slurping at my heated flesh.

The room begins to spin and darken around me. I grip his head to hold his mouth against me. My hips gently rock to his lapping rhythm.

"Yes—"

The tightening tickle builds in my belly. Every touch of his tongue edges me closer to my delirium. I'm falling deeper and deeper into the darkness of euphoria. A wail escapes me and my knees quiver, pulling me back from the deep pit of orgasm. I'm gasping for breath. My body jerks with each tap of his tongue on my twitching clit.

Jordan stands, wraps his arms around me and lifts me. He presses my back against the glass and pins me with his body. His hands grip my thighs while my arms wrap around his neck. My feet lock around his waist.

His towel falls to the floor as his cock plows it's full length into me. He fucks me as hard as he can as our mouths mesh together in an erotic, heated rage.

He sets me on my feet and spins me to face the glass. He bends me slightly and rams himself into my depths.

I'm so fucking wet!

"Fuck me!" I beg.

Jordan grips my waist and spreads his feet. A plethora of punishing thrusts have me lost in another orgasm and then another, and yet another. My knees quiver, barely able to hold my weight.

He pulls his prick from me, grabs my wrist and nearly drags me to the bedroom. He flops on his back, pulling me with him.

I straddle him and lower myself while enveloping his steel-hard cock. I rock on him as his hands caress my breasts and tease my nipples. My clitoris drags on his belly with each thrust, pulling me closer and closer to the glorious darkness.

My eyes remain closed, allowing me to hide from reality while feeling the physical pleasures that spoil my flesh.

If I open my eyes and look down, and he's looking up at me, he'll steal away my broken heart. I don't deserve to be happy. I lied to David about my relationship with Jordan. I didn't tell him I had had a baby when he and I tried for so long, only to fail. Worse yet, I was driving the car when we crashed. He died because I didn't react fast enough to avoid the drunk driver. If I hadn't insisted on going to the dairy bar for ice cream that night, he'd still be here. He deserves to be alive, not me. I'm an awful person.

Jordan sits up, takes my nipple in his mouth and teases it perfectly. I wrap my arms around his head and hold it against my chest and sob as I edge closer toward orgasm.

I continue to ride him as tears stream down my cheeks. Whimpers escape me as peaceful darkness surrounds me. An exquisite calmness fills my mind as a crashing orgasm rips through every cell in my physical form. This is my escape from the pain I hold within me.

As it slips away, I ride him faster while crying out, hoping to reclaim the euphoria.

Jordan wails as he dumps his seed deep inside me.

Once again, my grief overwhelms me when reality awakens.

Chapter Seven

The night is quick to claim me, pulling me into a deep sleep. I dream of David.

We're in the car, and it's that dreadful night. I'm begging him to let me turn the car around so we can go home. I know what's about to happen.

He's calm when he speaks. "Ally, you can't change the past. You have to accept it and move forward."

I try to hit the brakes, but it continues barrelling toward the oncoming lights.

"Please, David! You'll die!"

My panic has me trying to shut off the car, put it in park, slam the brakes, but nothing stops us from racing down the highway.

His voice soothes amongst the chaos. "I was never meant to be with you forever. Enjoy the time we had and move forward in life. Jordan is waiting for you."

Just before the oncoming lights hit us head-on, taking him from me again, everything freezes.

He leans toward me and kisses my lips tenderly. "Let me go."

The cars crash in a whirlwind of chaos.

I jolt straight up in the bed, gasping and covered in sweat, my heart pounds as if trying to escape my chest.

I hear dishes rattle in the kitchen and smell bacon frying on the stove.

A sense of calm overwhelms me and my heartbeat stills as if time has paused.

I hear David's voice. *"Ally, let me go. Jordan is a good man and he loves you. The child growing in your womb will need its father."*

I sit at the edge of the bed and listen to the calm beating of my heart.

David is gone. I'm alive.

I allow only a few more tears to fall for David. I wipe them away and make the decision to let him rest.

I stand, place a hand on my tummy and wonder if what David said is true. Am I pregnant?

The bedroom door slowly opens.

"I was wondering if you were planning on sleeping all day," Jordan says with a smile.

"No… I've been asleep far too long and it's time I wake up. I have the rest of my life to live."

The End

If you enjoyed Still Waters Burn Deep, please leave a review. The book can be found on all of the sites below.

Amazon
https://books2read.com/Still-Waters-Burn-Deep

Goodreads
https://www.goodreads.com/book/show/60183070-still-waters-burn-deep?from_search=true&from_srp=true&qid=oURrgPfPZM&rank=1

Bookbub
https://www.bookbub.com/books/still-waters-burn-deep-a-second-chance-short-story-romance-by-pebbles-lacasse

Allauthor.com
https://www.amazon.com/Still-Waters-Burn-Deep-Romance-ebook/dp/B09QX4S3WQ/ref=tmm_kin_swatch_0?_encoding=UTF8&qid=1642869688&sr=1-1

About the Author

Pebbles Lacasse is a contemporary romance and erotica author. She leans toward writing bad boys desiring women who didn't know they have a kinky side. However, she's also known for her women with a dominant  nature, and a secret yearning to be loved. Her books and short stories often take her readers into the BDSM lifestyle while revolving around real-life issues, and there's always a happy ending. The captivating stories of romance, love, and tender moments keep her readers coming back for more.

As someone living with Porphyria, Pebbles stays indoors to avoid UV light which gives her plenty of time to write. That's not to say she doesn't love "glamping," fishing, kayaking, and swimming, she just has to do it with protective clothing. If there's something she wants to do, she'll find a way to make it happen.

Pebbles Lacasse

Pebbles is very family oriented. She and her husband of 30+ years raised their children in southern Ontario where she was born, and remains to this day. A 150+ lbs Mastiff takes up a lot of room in their home and in their hearts. His best friends are the two rescue cats that think they rule the home. The chickens couldn't care less about the dog until he chases them when they come too close to his outdoor toys.

Discover more about Pebbles on her website
https://www.pebbleslacasse.com

Free short story with newsletter subscription:
https://bit.ly/pebbleskinkynews

<u>Keep swiping for more books you may enjoy!</u>

More Books by Pebbles Lacasse

Full Novels & Series
My Wife and Master Jake
Broken Charm

The Complete My JoeSmith Collection Boxed Set:
    My JoeSmith: Anonymity, Book One
    My JoeSmith: Anonymity, Book Two
    My JoeSmith: Nurture, Book Three
    My JoeSmith: Unity, Book Four
The Coaching Rayna Two Book Series:
    Coaching Rayna, Book One
    Coaching Rayna: Bound Hearts, Book Two
The Naughty Goldie Series:
    Goldilocks & The Three Bear Brothers, Book One
    Goldilocks & The Three Bear Brothers: Trifecta,
Book Two
    Goldilocks & The Three Bear Brothers: Overture,
Book Three
    Goldilocks & The Three Bear Brothers, Book Four

Short Stories
Little Miss Muffet
Hello Officer
Mistress Rabbit
A Run with Charley

Carter's Mistress
Still Waters Burn Deep
Dominatrix for Hire

Anthologies

Quarantined: A Boxed Set of Pandemic Proportions –
Still Waters Burn Deep

To read teasers and see book cover photoshoot photos
by Pebbles, visit **https://www.PebblesLacasse.com**

Connect with Pebbles

Facebook
https://www.facebook.com/PebblesLacasseEroticRomanceWriter/

Facebook Group
www.facebook.com/groups/pebbleslacasseandfriendsgroup/

Newsletter sign-up
https://bit.ly/pebbleskinkynews

Website
https://www.pebbleslacasse.com

Instagram
https://www.instagram.com/pebbleslacasse/

Twitter
https://twitter.com/pebbleslacasse

Goodreads
http://bit.ly/Goodreads_2y5xJji

Bookbub
https://www.bookbub.com/profile/pebbles-lacasse

Amazon
https://www.amazon.com/author/pebbleslacasse

Pebbles Lacasse

Youtube
https://www.youtube.com/channel/UC3Jb8ofSw0m
3TFn4cMWu5dw

TikTok
https://shorturl.at/SOzO8

Subscribe to Pebbles' Newsletter

Sign up to receive Pebbles Lacasse's newsletter and receive a free short story to welcome you. Be among the first to read teasers from the books she's writing, learn what Pebbles does to keep her busy when she isn't writing her steamy novels, discover the captivating authors she's reading, be led to books with similar genres grouped together just for readers like you, and other crazy antics.

https://bit.ly/pebbleskinkynews

Join Pebbles' Team

Would you like to be a valued member of my **_ARC team_**? Advanced Readers receive copies of my soon-to-be published novels to read with the promise to leave reviews by the date set by Pebbles.
*You'll get **my books for FREE** forever as long as you leave reviews!*
Sound like a good deal?

https://forms.gle/wyq53oMdbWSG574f8

www.PebblesLacasse.com
Erotic Romance Writer

www.ingramcontent.com/pod-product-compliance
Lightning Source LLC
Chambersburg PA
CBHW070356130626
46556CB00007B/3190